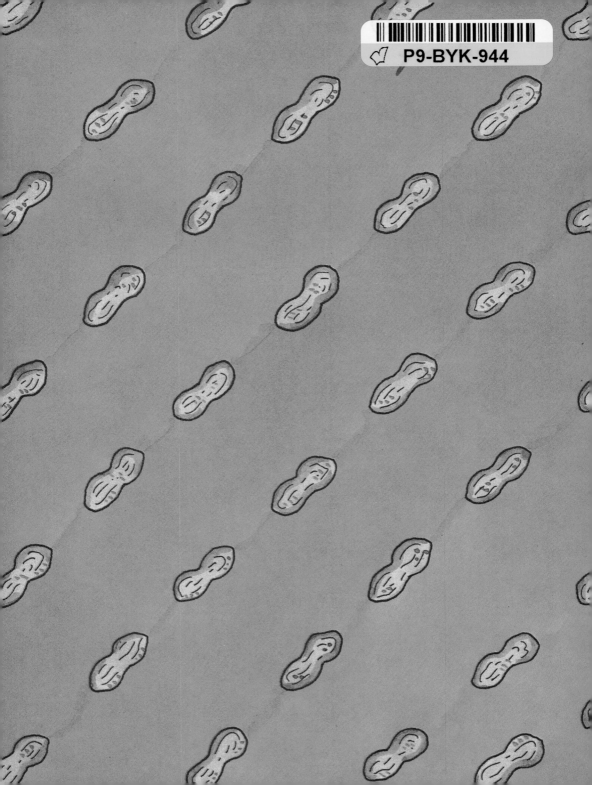

Aren't You Forgetting Something, Fiona?

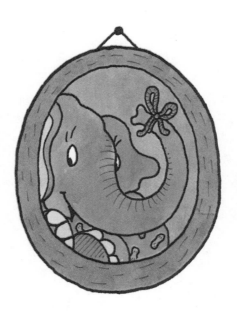

A Parents Magazine
Read Aloud Original

Aren't You Forgetting Something, Fiona?

by Joanna Cole
pictures by Ned Delaney

Parents Magazine Press
New York

To Shaina Feinberg—J.C.

To Bob Longley—N.D.

Text copyright © 1983 by Joanna Cole
Illustrations copyright © 1983 by Thomas N. Delaney III
All rights reserved.
Printed in the United States of America.
10 9 8 7 6 5 4 3

Library of Congress Cataloging in Publication Data
Cole, Joanna
Aren't You Forgetting Something, Fiona?
Summary: With the help of her family, Fiona, who has
trouble remembering even the simplest things, remembers
to go to exercise class with her best friend.
(1. Memory—Fiction.   2. Elephants—Fiction)
I. Delaney, Ned, ill.   II. Title
PZ7.C67346Ar   1983 [E]   83-13457
ISBN 0-8193-1121-9

Aren't You Forgetting Something, Fiona?

In Fiona's family everyone was
good at remembering things.
Everyone except Fiona.

Fiona's mother always remembered where she put things.

Fiona's father remembered all his
Aunt Sophie's best recipes.

Fiona's grandmother remembered
the words to every song she ever heard.

And Fiona's brother, Tim, remembered
every bad thing Fiona had ever done to him.

But Fiona had trouble remembering
even the simplest things.

If her mother asked her to get one thing,

she came back with something else.

Even when she went out to play, Fiona was forgetful.

One day Fiona signed up for
an exercise class with
her best friend, Felicity.

But the day before class,
Fiona began to worry.

What if she forgot her gym clothes?
What if she forgot to go to class at all?
Fiona decided to ask her family for help.

"Make a big X on the calendar to remind yourself which day it is," said Tim.

"Put a note up telling yourself to go to class," said Grandmother. "Leave your gym bag by the door," said Father.

"And tie a ribbon around your trunk," said Mother. "Every time you see the ribbon, it will remind you that there is something special to remember."

Fiona did it all.

The next morning she saw the X,
read the note, picked up her bag,
and left the house right after breakfast.

But it was too good to last.
Fiona forgot where she was going.
She went up one street and down another.

Then she noticed the ribbon on her trunk.
"If I am wearing a ribbon, I must be
going to a party," thought Fiona.
"Maybe it is Felicity's birthday."

Fiona ran to the store for a present.
Then she set out for Felicity's house.

She hadn't gone far when she saw
Felicity poke her head out a window.
Then Fiona remembered her gym class.

Fiona gave Felicity the present anyway.
"My birthday isn't until next month,"
said Felicity. "But thank you, Fiona."

The present made jumping exercises
a lot more fun. And Fiona's ribbon
made a great headband.

Knee bend

That night, Fiona showed her family
what she'd learned in class.
She remembered everything.

Handstand

Pushup

Jumping jack

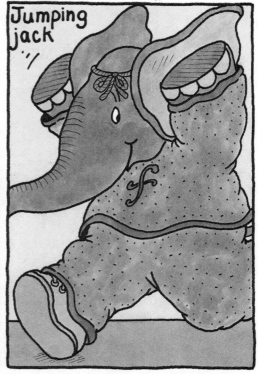

High kick

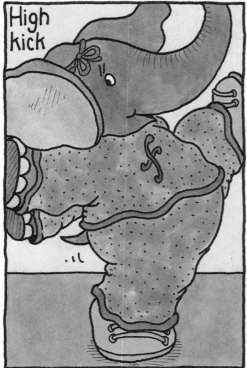

Backward roll

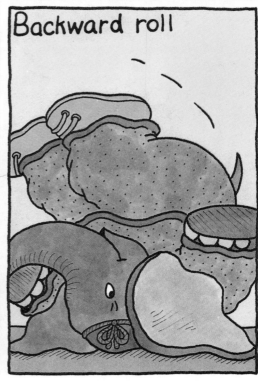

Her family was very proud of her.

And Fiona was proud of herself.

She went off happily to take her bath
and get ready for bed.
It had been a fine day—
one Fiona would remember for a long time!

About the Author

JOANNA COLE usually has a good memory. But once, before going on vacation, she hid some valuable jewelry in a safe place. When she came back she forgot where she had hidden it. In fact, she forgot she owned it! One year later, while cleaning out a cupboard, she was happily surprised to find it. "I like to think that, like Fiona, I remember the important things," she says.

Joanna Cole writes books for and about children. She lives in New York City with her husband and daughter.

About the Artist

NED DELANEY has been writing and illustrating picture books since he graduated from college. He also teaches writing and illustrating at Salem State College in the Boston area, where he lives.

Like Joanna Cole, Mr. Delaney says he usually has a good memory. But he admits, "As I was packing up the art for this book, I found I had forgotten to draw the ribbons on Fiona's trunk!" As you can see though, he remembered in time and all the ribbons are just where they should be.

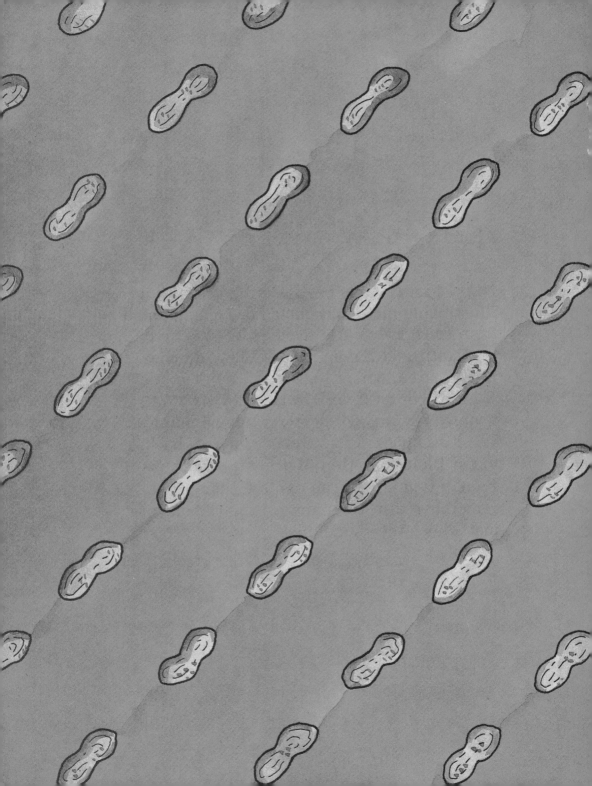